The Author of Beltraffio

Henry James

Contents

THE AUTHOR OF BELTRAFFIO

BY

Henry James

CHAPTER I

Much as I wished to see him I had kept my letter of introduction three weeks in my pocket-book. I was nervous and timid about meeting him--conscious of youth and ignorance, convinced that he was tormented by strangers, and especially by my country-people, and not exempt from the suspicion that he had the irritability as well as the dignity of genius. Moreover, the pleasure, if it should occur--for I could scarcely believe it was near at hand--would be so great that I wished to think of it in advance, to feel it there against my breast, not to mix it with satisfactions more superficial and usual. In the little game of new sensations that I was playing with my ingenuous mind I wished to keep my visit to the author of "Beltraffio" as a trump-card. It was three years after the publication of that fascinating work, which I had read over five times and which now, with my riper judgement, I admire on the whole as much as ever. This will give you about the date of my first visit--of any duration--to England for you will not have forgotten the commotion, I may even say the scandal, produced by Mark Ambient's masterpiece. It was the most complete presentation that had yet been made of the gospel of art; it was a kind of aesthetic war-cry. People had endeavoured to sail nearer to "truth" in the cut of their sleeves and the shape of their sideboards; but there had not as yet been, among English novels, such an example of beauty of execution and "intimate" importance of theme. Nothing had been done in that line from the point of view of art for art. That served me as a fond formula, I may mention, when I was twenty-five; how much it still serves I won't take upon myself to say--especially as the discerning reader will be able to judge for himself. I had been in England, briefly, a twelve-month before the time to which I began by alluding, and had then learned that Mr. Ambient was in distant lands--was making a considerable tour in the East; so that there was nothing to do but to keep my letter till I should be in London again. It was of little use to me to hear that his wife had not left England and was, with her little boy, their only child, spending the period of her husband's absence--a good many months--at a small place they had down in Surrey. They had a house in London, but actually in the occupation of other persons. All this I had picked up, and also that Mrs. Ambient was charming--my friend the American poet, from whom I had my introduction, had never seen her, his relations with the great man confined to the exchange of letters; but she wasn't, after all, though she had lived so near the rose, the author of "Beltraffio," and I didn't go down into Surrey to call on her. I went to the Continent, spent the following winter in Italy, and returned to London in May. My visit to Italy had opened my eyes to a good many things, but to nothing more than the beauty of certain pages in the works of Mark Ambient. I carried his productions about in my trunk--they are not, as you know, very numerous, but he had preluded to "Beltraffio" by, some exquisite things--and I used to read them over in the evening at the inn. I used profoundly to reason that the man who drew those characters and wrote that style understood what he saw and knew what he was doing. This is my sole ground for mentioning my winter in Italy. He had been there much in former years--he was saturated with what painters call the "feeling" of that classic land. He expressed the charm of the old hill-cities of Tuscany, the look of certain lonely grass-grown places which, in the past, had echoed with life; he understood the great artists, he understood the spirit of the Renaissance; he understood everything. The scene of one of his earlier novels was laid in Rome, the scene of another in Florence, and I had moved through these cities in company with the figures he set so firmly on their feet. This is why I was now so much happier even than before in the prospect of making his acquaintance.

At last, when I had dallied with my privilege long enough, I despatched to him the missive of the American poet. He had already gone out of town; he shrank from the rigour of the London "season" and it was his habit to migrate on the first of June. Moreover I had heard he was this year hard at work on a new book, into which some of his impressions of the East were to be wrought, so that he desired nothing so much as quiet days. That knowledge, however, didn't prevent me--cet age est sans pitie--from sending with my friend's letter a note of my own, in which I asked his leave to come down and see him for an hour or two on some day to be named by himself. My proposal was accompanied with a very frank expression of my sentiments, and the effect of the entire appeal was to elicit from the great man the kindest possible invitation. He would be delighted to see me, especially if I should turn up on the following Saturday and would remain till the Monday morning. We would take a walk over the Surrey commons, and I could tell him all about the other great man, the one in America. He indicated to me the best train, and it may be imagined whether on the Saturday afternoon I was punctual at Waterloo. He carried his benevolence to the point of coming to meet me at the little station at which I was to alight, and my heart beat very fast as I saw his handsome face, surmounted with a soft wide-awake and which I knew by a photograph long since enshrined on my mantel-shelf, scanning the carriage-windows as the train rolled up. He recognised me as infallibly as I had recognised himself; he appeared to know by instinct how a young American of critical pretensions, rash youth, would look when much divided between eagerness and modesty. He took me by the hand and smiled at me and said: "You must be--a--YOU, I think!" and asked if I should mind going on foot to his house, which would take but a few minutes. I remember feeling it a piece of extraordinary affability that he should give directions about the conveyance of my bag; I remember feeling altogether very happy and rosy, in fact quite transported, when he laid his hand on my shoulder as we came out of the station.

I surveyed him, askance, as we walked together; I had already, I had indeed instantly, seen him as all delightful. His face is so well known that I needn't describe it; he looked to me at once an English gentleman and a man of genius, and I thought that a happy combination. There was a brush of the Bohemian in his fineness; you would easily have guessed his belonging to the artist guild. He was addicted to velvet jackets, to cigarettes, to loose shirt-collars, to looking a little dishevelled. His features, which were firm but not perfectly regular, are fairly enough represented in his portraits; but no portrait I have seen gives any idea of his expression. There were innumerable things in it, and they chased each other in and out of his face. I have seen people who were grave and gay in quick alternation; but Mark Ambient was grave and gay at one and the same moment. There were other strange oppositions and contradictions in his slightly faded and fatigued countenance. He affected me somehow as at once fresh and stale, at once anxious and indifferent. He had evidently had an active past, which inspired one with curiosity; yet what was that compared to his obvious future? He was just enough above middle height to be spoken of as tall, and rather lean and long in the flank.   He had the friendliest frankest manner possible, and yet I could see it cost him something.   It cost him small spasms of the self-consciousness that is an Englishman's last and dearest treasure--the thing he pays his way through life by sacrificing small pieces of even as the gallant but moneyless adventurer in "Quentin Durward" broke off links of his brave gold chain.   He had been thirty-eight years old at the time "Beltraffio" was published.   He asked me about his friend in America, about the length of my stay in England, about the last news in London and the people I had seen there; and I remember looking for the signs of genius in the very form of his questions and thinking I found it.   I liked his voice as if I were somehow myself having the use of it.

There was genius in his house too I thought when we got there; there was imagination in the carpets and curtains, in the pictures and books, in the garden behind it, where certain old brown walls were muffled in creepers that appeared to me to have been copied from a masterpiece of one of the pre-Raphaelites.   That was the way many things struck me at that time, in England--as reproductions of something that existed primarily in art or literature.   It was not the picture, the poem, the fictive page, that seemed to me a copy; these things were the originals, and the life of happy and distinguished people was fashioned in their image.   Mark Ambient called his house a cottage, and I saw afterwards he was right for if it hadn't been a cottage it must have been a villa, and a villa, in England at least, was not a place in which one could fancy him at home.   But it was, to my vision, a cottage glorified and translated; it was a palace of art, on a slightly reduced scale--and might besides have been the dearest haunt of the old English genius loci. It nestled under a cluster of magnificent beeches, it had little creaking lattices that opened out of, or into, pendent mats of ivy, and gables, and old red tiles, as well as a general aspect of being painted in water-colours and inhabited by people whose lives would go on in chapters and volumes. The lawn seemed to me of extraordinary extent, the garden-walls of incalculable height, the whole air of the place delightfully still, private, proper to itself. "My wife must be somewhere about," Mark Ambient said as we went in. "We shall find her perhaps--we've about an hour before dinner. She may be in the garden. I'll show you my little place."

We passed through the house and into the grounds, as I should have called them, which extended into the rear. They covered scarce three or four acres, but, like the house, were very old and crooked and full of traces of long habitation, with inequalities of level and little flights of steps--mossy and cracked were these--which connected the different parts with each other. The limits of the place, cleverly dissimulated, were muffled in the great verdurous screens. They formed, as I remember, a thick loose curtain at the further end, in one of the folds of which, as it were, we presently made out from afar a little group. "Ah there she is!" said Mark Ambient; "and she has got the boy." He noted that last fact in a slightly different tone from any in which he yet had spoken. I wasn't fully aware of this at the time, but it lingered in my ear and I afterwards understood it.

"Is it your son?" I inquired, feeling the question not to be brilliant.

"Yes, my only child. He's always in his mother's pocket. She coddles him too much." It came back to me afterwards too--the sound of these critical words. They weren't petulant; they expressed rather a sudden coldness, a mechanical submission. We went a few steps further, and then he stopped short and called the boy, beckoning to him repeatedly.

"Dolcino, come and see your daddy!" There was something in the way he stood still and waited that made me think he did it for a purpose.

Mrs. Ambient had her arm round the child's waist, and he was leaning against her knee; but though he moved at his father's call she gave no sign of releasing him. A lady, apparently a neighbour, was seated near her, and before them was a garden-table on which a tea- service had been placed.

Mark Ambient called again, and Dolcino struggled in the maternal embrace; but, too tightly held, he after two or three fruitless efforts jerked about and buried his head deep in his mother's lap. There was a certain awkwardness in the scene; I thought it odd Mrs. Ambient should pay so little attention to her husband. But I wouldn't for the world have betrayed my thought, and, to conceal it, I began loudly to rejoice in the prospect of our having tea in the garden. "Ah she won't let him come!" said my host with a sigh; and we went our way till we reached the two ladies. He mentioned my name to his wife, and I noticed that he addressed her as "My dear," very genially, without a trace of resentment at her detention of the child. The quickness of the transition made me vaguely ask myself if he were perchance henpecked--a shocking surmise which I instantly dismissed. Mrs. Ambient was quite such a wife as I should have expected him to have; slim and fair, with a long neck and pretty eyes and an air of good breeding. She shone with a certain coldness and practised in intercourse a certain bland detachment, but she was clothed in gentleness as in one of those vaporous redundant scarves that muffle the heroines of Gainsborough and Romney. She had also a vague air of race, justified by my afterwards learning that she was "connected with the aristocracy." I have seen poets married to women of whom it was difficult to conceive that they should gratify the poetic fancy--women with dull faces and glutinous minds, who were none the less, however, excellent wives. But there was no obvious disparity in Mark Ambient's union. My hostess--so far as she could be called so--delicate and quiet, in a white dress, with her beautiful child at her side, was worthy of the author of a work so distinguished as "Beltraffio." Round her neck she wore a black velvet ribbon, of which the long ends, tied behind, hung down her back, and to which, in front, was attached a miniature portrait of her little boy. Her smooth shining hair was confined in a net. She gave me an adequate greeting, and Dolcino--I thought this small name of endearment delightful--took advantage of her getting up to slip away from her and go to his father, who seized him in silence and held him high for a long moment, kissing him several times.

I had lost no time in observing that the child, not more than seven years old, was extraordinarily beautiful. He had the face of an angel-- the eyes, the hair, the smile of innocence, the more than mortal bloom. There was something that deeply touched, that almost alarmed, in his beauty, composed, one would have said, of elements too fine and pure for the breath of this world. When I spoke to him and he came and held out his hand and smiled at me I felt a sudden strange pity for him--quite as if he had been an orphan or a changeling or stamped with some social stigma. It was impossible to be in fact more exempt from these misfortunes, and yet, as one kissed him, it was hard to keep from murmuring all tenderly "Poor little devil!" though why one should have applied this epithet to a living cherub is more than I can say. Afterwards indeed I knew a trifle better; I grasped the truth of his being too fair to live, wondering at the same time that his parents shouldn't have guessed it and have been in proportionate grief and despair. For myself I had no doubt of his evanescence, having already more than once caught in the fact the particular infant charm that's as good as a death-warrant.

The lady who had been sitting with Mrs. Ambient was a jolly ruddy personage in velveteen and limp feathers, whom I guessed to be the vicar's wife--our hostess didn't introduce me--and who immediately began to talk to Ambient about chrysanthemums. This was a safe subject, and yet there was a certain surprise for me in seeing the author of "Beltraffio" even in such superficial communion with the Church of England. His writings implied so much detachment from that institution, expressed a view of life so profane, as it were, so independent and so little likely in general to be thought edifying, that I should have expected to find him an object of horror to vicars and their ladies--of horror repaid on his own part by any amount of effortless derision. This proved how little I knew as yet of the English people and their extraordinary talent for keeping up their forms, as well as of some of the mysteries of Mark Ambient's hearth and home. I found afterwards that he had, in his study, between nervous laughs and free cigar-puffs, some wonderful comparisons for his clerical neighbours; but meanwhile the chrysanthemums were a source of harmony, he and the vicaress were equally attached to them, and I was surprised at the knowledge they exhibited of this interesting plant. The lady's visit, however, had presumably been long, and she presently rose for departure and kissed Mrs. Ambient. Mark started to walk with her to the gate of the grounds, holding Dolcino by the hand.

"Stay with me, darling," Mrs. Ambient said to the boy, who had surrendered himself to his father.

Mark paid no attention to the summons but Dolcino turned and looked at her in shy appeal, "Can't I go with papa?"

"Not when I ask you to stay with me."

"But please don't ask me, mamma," said the child in his small clear new voice.

"I must ask you when I want you. Come to me, dearest." And Mrs. Ambient, who had seated herself again, held out her long slender slightly too osseous hands.

Her husband stopped, his back turned to her, but without releasing the child. He was still talking to the vicaress, but this good lady, I think, had lost the thread of her attention. She looked at Mrs. Ambient and at Dolcino, and then looked at me, smiling in a highly amused cheerful manner and almost to a grimace.

"Papa," said the child, "mamma wants me not to go with you."

"He's very tired--he has run about all day. He ought to be quiet till he goes to bed. Otherwise he won't sleep." These declarations fell successively and very distinctly from Mrs. Ambient's lips.

Her husband, still without turning round, bent over the boy and looked at him in silence. The vicaress gave a genial irrelevant laugh and observed that he was a precious little pet. "Let him choose," said Mark Ambient. "My dear little boy, will you go with me or will you stay with your mother?"

"Oh it's a shame!" cried the vicar's lady with increased hilarity.

"Papa, I don't think I can choose," the child answered, making his voice very low and confidential. "But I've been a great deal with mamma to-day," he then added.

"And very little with papa! My dear fellow, I think you HAVE chosen!" On which Mark Ambient walked off with his son, accompanied by re-echoing but inarticulate comments from my fellow-visitor.

His wife had seated herself again, and her fixed eyes, bent on the ground, expressed for a few moments so much mute agitation that anything I could think of to say would be but a false note. Yet she none the less quickly recovered herself, to express the sufficiently civil hope that I didn't mind having had to walk from the station. I reassured her on this point, and she went on: "We've got a thing that might have gone for you, but my husband wouldn't order it." After which and another longish pause, broken only by my plea that the pleasure of a walk with our friend would have been quite what I would have chosen, she found for reply: "I believe the Americans walk very little."

"Yes, we always run," I laughingly allowed.

She looked at me seriously, yet with an absence in her pretty eyes. "I suppose your distances are so great."

"Yes, but we break our marches! I can't tell you the pleasure to me of finding myself here," I added. "I've the greatest admiration for Mr. Ambient."

"He'll like that. He likes being admired."

"He must have a very happy life, then. He has many worshippers."

"Oh yes, I've seen some of them," she dropped, looking away, very far from me, rather as if such a vision were before her at the moment. It seemed to indicate, her tone, that the sight was scarcely edifying, and I guessed her quickly enough to be in no great intellectual sympathy with the author of "Beltraffio." I thought the fact strange, but somehow, in the glow of my own enthusiasm, didn't think it important it only made me wish rather to emphasise that homage.

"For me, you know," I returned--doubtless with a due suffisance-- "he's quite the greatest of living writers."

"Of course I can't judge. Of course he's very clever," she said with a patient cheer.

"He's nothing less than supreme, Mrs. Ambient! There are pages in each of his books of a perfection classing them with the greatest things. Accordingly for me to see him in this familiar way, in his habit as he lives, and apparently to find the man as delightful as the artist--well, I can't tell you how much too good to be true it seems and how great a privilege I think it." I knew I was gushing, but I couldn't help it, and what I said was a good deal less than what I felt. I was by no means sure I should dare to say even so much as this to the master himself, and there was a kind of rapture in speaking it out to his wife which was not affected by the fact that, as a wife, she appeared peculiar. She listened to me with her face grave again and her lips a little compressed, listened as if in no doubt, of course, that her husband was remarkable, but as if at the same time she had heard it frequently enough and couldn't treat it as stirring news. There was even in her manner a suggestion that I was so young as to expose myself to being called forward--an imputation and a word I had always loathed; as well as a hinted reminder that people usually got over their early extravagance. "I assure you that for me this is a red-letter day," I added.

She didn't take this up, but after a pause, looking round her, said abruptly and a trifle dryly: "We're very much afraid about the fruit this year."

My eyes wandered to the mossy mottled garden-walls, where plum-trees and pears, flattened and fastened upon the rusty bricks, looked like crucified figures with many arms. "Doesn't it promise well?"

"No, the trees look very dull. We had such late frosts."

Then there was another pause. She addressed her attention to the opposite end of the grounds, kept it for her husband's return with the child. "Is Mr. Ambient fond of gardening?" it occurred to me to ask, irresistibly impelled as I felt myself, moreover, to bring the conversation constantly back to him.

"He's very fond of plums," said his wife.

"Ah well, then, I hope your crop will be better than you fear. It's a lovely old place," I continued. "The whole impression's that of certain places he has described. Your house is like one of his pictures."

She seemed a bit frigidly amused at my glow. "It's a pleasant little place. There are hundreds like it."

"Oh it has his TONE," I laughed, but sounding my epithet and insisting on my point the more sharply that my companion appeared to see in my appreciation of her simple establishment a mark of mean experience.

It was clear I insisted too much. "His tone?" she repeated with a harder look at me and a slightly heightened colour.

"Surely he has a tone, Mrs. Ambient."

"Oh yes, he has indeed! But I don't in the least consider that I'm living in one of his books at all. I shouldn't care for that in the least," she went on with a smile that had in some degree the effect of converting her really sharp protest into an insincere joke. "I'm afraid I'm not very literary. And I'm not artistic," she stated.

"I'm very sure you're not ignorant, not stupid," I ventured to reply, with the accompaniment of feeling immediately afterwards that I had been both familiar and patronising. My only consolation was in the sense that she had begun it, had fairly dragged me into it. She had thrust forward her limitations.

"Well, whatever I am I'm very different from my husband. If you like him you won't like me. You needn't say anything. Your liking me isn't in the least necessary!"

"Don't defy me!" I could but honourably make answer.

She looked as if she hadn't heard me, which was the best thing she could do; and we sat some time without further speech. Mrs. Ambient had evidently the enviable English quality of being able to be mute without unrest. But at last she spoke--she asked me if there seemed many people in town. I gave her what satisfaction I could on this point, and we talked a little of London and of some of its characteristics at that time of the year. At the end of this I came back irrepressibly to Mark.

"Doesn't he like to be there now? I suppose he doesn't find the proper quiet for his work. I should think his things had been written for the most part in a very still place. They suggest a great stillness following on a kind of tumult. Don't you think so?" I laboured on. "I suppose London's a tremendous place to collect impressions, but a refuge like this, in the country, must be better for working them up. Does he get many of his impressions in London, should you say?" I proceeded from point to point in this malign inquiry simply because my hostess, who probably thought me an odious chattering person, gave me time; for when I paused--I've not represented my pauses--she simply continued to let her eyes wander while her long fair fingers played with the medallion on her neck. When I stopped altogether, however, she was obliged to say something, and what she said was that she hadn't the least idea where her husband got his impressions. This made me think her, for a moment, positively disagreeable; delicate and proper and rather aristocratically fine as she sat there. But I must either have lost that view a moment later or been goaded by it to further aggression, for I remember asking her if our great man were in a good vein of work and when we might look for the appearance of the book on which he was engaged. I've every reason now to know that she found me insufferable.

She gave a strange small laugh as she said: "I'm afraid you think I know much more about my husband's work than I do. I haven't the least idea what he's doing," she then added in a slightly different, that is a more explanatory, tone and as if from a glimpse of the enormity of her confession. "I don't read what he writes."

She didn't succeed, and wouldn't even had she tried much harder, in making this seem to me anything less than monstrous. I stared at her and I think I blushed. "Don't you admire his genius? Don't you admire 'Beltraffio'?"

She waited, and I wondered what she could possibly say. She didn't speak, I could see, the first words that rose to her lips; she repeated what she had said a few minutes before. "Oh of course he's very clever!" And with this she got up; our two absentees had reappeared.

CHAPTER II

Mrs. Ambient left me and went to meet them; she stopped and had a few words with her husband that I didn't hear and that ended in her taking the child by the hand and returning with him to the house. Her husband joined me in a moment, looking, I thought, the least bit conscious and constrained, and said that if I would come in with him he would show me my room. In looking back upon these first moments of my visit I find it important to avoid the error of appearing to have at all fully measured his situation from the first or made out the signs of things mastered only afterwards. This later knowledge throws a backward light and makes me forget that, at least on the occasion of my present reference--I mean that first afternoon--Mark Ambient struck me as only enviable. Allowing for this he must yet have failed of much expression as we walked back to the house, though I remember well the answer he made to a remark of mine on his small son.

"That's an extraordinary little boy of yours. I've never seen such a child."

"Why," he asked while we went, "do you call him extraordinary?"

"He's so beautiful, so fascinating. He's like some perfect little work of art."

He turned quickly in the passage, grasping my arm. "Oh don't call him that, or you'll--you'll--!"

But in his hesitation he broke off suddenly, laughing at my surprise. Immediately afterwards, however, he added: "You'll make his little future very difficult."

I declared that I wouldn't for the world take any liberties with his little future--it seemed to me to hang by threads of such delicacy. I should only be highly interested in watching it.

"You Americans are very keen," he commented on this. "You notice more things than we do."

"Ah if you want visitors who aren't struck with you," I cried, "you shouldn't have asked me down here!"

He showed me my room, a little bower of chintz, with open windows where the light was green, and before he left me said irrelevantly: "As for my small son, you know, we shall probably kill him between us before we've done with him!" And he made this assertion as if he really believed it, without any appearance of jest, his fine near- sighted expressive eyes looking straight into mine.

"Do you mean by spoiling him?"

"No, by fighting for him!"

"You had better give him to me to keep for you," I said. "Let me remove the apple of discord!"

It was my extravagance of course, but he had the air of being perfectly serious. "It would be quite the best thing we could do. I should be all ready to do it."

"I'm greatly obliged to you for your confidence."

But he lingered with his hands in his pockets. I felt as if within a few moments I had, morally speaking, taken several steps nearer to him. He looked weary, just as he faced me then, looked preoccupied and as if there were something one might do for him. I was terribly conscious of the limits of my young ability, but I wondered what such a service might be, feeling at bottom nevertheless that the only thing I could do for him was to like him. I suppose he guessed this and was grateful for what was in my mind, since he went on presently: "I haven't the advantage of being an American, but I also notice a little, and I've an idea that"--here he smiled and laid his hand on my shoulder--"even counting out your nationality you're not destitute of intelligence. I've only known you half an hour, but--!" For which again he pulled up. "You're very young, after all."

"But you may treat me as if I could understand you!" I said; and before he left me to dress for dinner he had virtually given me a promise that he would.

When I went down into the drawing-room--I was very punctual--I found that neither my hostess nor my host had appeared. A lady rose from a sofa, however, and inclined her head as I rather surprisedly gazed at her. "I daresay you don't know me," she said with the modern laugh. "I'm Mark Ambient's sister." Whereupon I shook hands with her, saluting her very low. Her laugh was modern--by which I mean that it consisted of the vocal agitation serving between people who meet in drawing-rooms as the solvent of social disparities, the medium of transitions; but her appearance was--what shall I call it?--medieval. She was pale and angular, her long thin face was inhabited by sad dark eyes and her black hair intertwined with golden fillets and curious clasps. She wore a faded velvet robe which clung to her when she moved and was "cut," as to the neck and sleeves, like the garments of old Italians. She suggested a symbolic picture, something akin even to Durer's Melancholia, and was so perfect an image of a type which I, in my ignorance, supposed to be extinct, that while she rose before me I was almost as much startled as if I had seen a ghost. I afterwards concluded that Miss

Ambient wasn't incapable of deriving pleasure from this weird effect, and I now believe that reflexion concerned in her having sunk again to her seat with her long lean but not ungraceful arms locked together in an archaic manner on her knees and her mournful eyes addressing me a message of intentness which foreshadowed what I was subsequently to suffer. She was a singular fatuous artificial creature, and I was never more than half to penetrate her motives and mysteries. Of one thing I'm sure at least: that they were considerably less insuperable than her appearance announced. Miss Ambient was a restless romantic disappointed spinster, consumed with the love of Michael-Angelesque attitudes and mystical robes; but I'm now convinced she hadn't in her nature those depths of unutterable thought which, when you first knew her, seemed to look out from her eyes and to prompt her complicated gestures. Those features in especial had a misleading eloquence; they lingered on you with a far- off dimness, an air of obstructed sympathy, which was certainly not always a key to the spirit of their owner; so that, of a truth, a young lady could scarce have been so dejected and disillusioned without having committed a crime for which she was consumed with remorse, or having parted with a hope that she couldn't sanely have entertained. She had, I believe, the usual allowance of rather vain motives: she wished to be looked at, she wished to be married, she wished to be thought original.

It costs me a pang to speak in this irreverent manner of one of Ambient's name, but I shall have still less gracious things to say before I've finished my anecdote, and moreover--I confess it--I owe the young lady a bit of a grudge. Putting aside the curious cast of her face she had no natural aptitude for an artistic development, had little real intelligence. But her affectations rubbed off on her brother's renown, and as there were plenty of people who darkly disapproved of him they could easily point to his sister as a person formed by his influence. It was quite possible to regard her as a warning, and she had almost compromised him with the world at large. He was the original and she the inevitable imitation. I suppose him scarce aware of the impression she mainly produced, beyond having a general idea that she made up very well as a Rossetti; he was used to her and was sorry for her, wishing she would marry and observing how she didn't. Doubtless I take her too seriously, for she did me no harm, though I'm bound to allow that I can only half-account for her. She wasn't so mystical as she looked, but was a strange indirect uncomfortable embarrassing woman. My story gives the reader at best so very small a knot to untie that I needn't hope to excite his curiosity by delaying to remark that Mrs. Ambient hated her sister- in-law. This I learned but later on, when other matters came to my knowledge. I mention it, however, at once, for I shall perhaps not seem to count too much on having beguiled him if I say he must promptly have guessed it. Mrs. Ambient, a person of conscience, put the best face on her kinswoman, who spent a month with her twice a year; but it took no great insight to recognise the very different personal paste of the two ladies, and that the usual feminine hypocrisies would cost them on either side much more than the usual effort. Mrs. Ambient, smooth-haired, thin-lipped, perpetually fresh, must have regarded her crumpled and dishevelled visitor as an equivocal joke; she herself so the opposite of a Rossetti, she herself a Reynolds or a Lawrence, with no more far-fetched note in her composition than a cold ladylike candour and a well-starched muslin dress.

It was in a garment and with an expression of this kind that she made her entrance after I had exchanged a few words with Miss Ambient. Her husband presently followed her and, there being no other company, we went to dinner. The impressions I received at that repast are present to me still. The elements of oddity in the air hovered, as it were, without descending--to any immediate check of my delight. This came mainly, of course, from Ambient's talk, the easiest and richest I had ever heard. I mayn't say to-day whether he laid himself out to dazzle a rather juvenile pilgrim from over the sea; but that matters little--it seemed so natural to him to shine. His spoken wit or wisdom, or whatever, had thus a charm almost beyond his written; that is if the high finish of his printed prose be really, as some people have maintained, a fault. There was such a kindness in him, however, that I've no doubt it gave him ideas for me, or about me, to see me sit as open-mouthed as I now figure myself. Not so the two ladies, who not only were very nearly dumb from beginning to end of the meal, but who hadn't even the air of being struck with such an exhibition of fancy and taste. Mrs. Ambient, detached, and inscrutable, met neither my eye nor her husband's; she attended to her dinner, watched her servants, arranged the puckers in her dress, exchanged at wide intervals a remark with her sister-in-law and, while she slowly rubbed her lean white hands between the courses, looked out of the window at the first signs of evening--the long June day allowing us to dine without candles. Miss Ambient appeared to give little direct heed to anything said by her brother; but on the other hand she was much engaged in watching its effect upon me. Her "die-away" pupils continued to attach themselves to my countenance, and it was only her air of belonging to another century that kept them from being importunate. She seemed to look at me across the ages, and the interval of time diminished for me the inconvenience. It was as if she knew in a general way that he must be talking very well, but she herself was so at home among such allusions that she had no need to pick them up and was at liberty to see what would become of the exposure of a candid young American to a high aesthetic temperature.

The temperature was aesthetic certainly, but it was less so than I could have desired, for I failed of any great success in making our friend abound about himself. I tried to put him on the ground of his own genius, but he slipped through my fingers every time and shifted the saddle to one or other of his contemporaries. He talked about Balzac and Browning, about what was being done in foreign countries, about his recent tour in the East and the extraordinary forms of life to be observed in that part of the world. I felt he had reasons for holding off from a direct profession of literary faith, a full consistency or sincerity, and therefore dealt instead with certain social topics, treating them with extraordinary humour and with a due play of that power of ironic evocation in which his books abound. He had a deal to say about London as London appears to the observer who has the courage of some of his conclusions during the high-pressure time--from April to July--of its gregarious life. He flashed his faculty of playing with the caught image and liberating the wistful idea over the whole scheme of manners or conception of intercourse of his compatriots, among whom there were evidently not a few types for which he had little love. London in short was grotesque to him, and he made capital sport of it; his only allusion that I can remember to his own work was his saying that he meant some day to do an immense and general, a kind of epic, social satire. Miss Ambient's perpetual gaze seemed to put to me: "Do you perceive how artistic, how very strange and interesting, we are? Frankly now is it possible to be MORE artistic, MORE strange and interesting, than this? You surely won't deny that we're remarkable." I was irritated by her use of the plural pronoun, for she had no right to pair herself with her brother; and moreover, of course, I couldn't see my way to--at all genially--include Mrs. Ambient. Yet there was no doubt they were, taken together, unprecedented enough, and, with all allowances, I had never been left, or condemned, to draw so many rich inferences.

After the ladies had retired my host took me into his study to smoke, where I appealingly brought him round, or so tried, to some disclosure of fond ideals. I was bent on proving I was worthy to listen to him, on repaying him for what he had said to me before dinner, by showing him how perfectly I understood. He liked to talk; he liked to defend his convictions and his honour (not that I attacked them); he liked a little perhaps--it was a pardonable weakness--to bewilder the youthful mind even while wishing to win it over. My ingenuous sympathy received at any rate a shock from three or four of his professions--he made me occasionally gasp and stare. He couldn't help forgetting, or rather couldn't know, how little, in another and drier clime, I had ever sat in the school in which he was master; and he promoted me as at a jump to a sense of its penetralia. My trepidations, however, were delightful; they were just what I had hoped for, and their only fault was that they passed away too quickly; since I found that for the main points I was essentially, I was quite constitutionally, on Mark Ambient's "side." This was the taken stand of the artist to whom every manifestation of human energy was a thrilling spectacle and who felt for ever the desire to resolve his experience of life into a literary form. On that high head of the passion for form the attempt at perfection, the quest for which was to his mind the real search for the holy grail--he said the most interesting, the most inspiring things. He mixed with them a thousand illustrations from his own life, from other lives he had known, from history and fiction, and above all from the annals of the time that was dear to him beyond all periods, the Italian cinque- cento. It came to me thus that in his books he had uttered but half his thought, and that what he had kept back from motives I deplored when I made them out later--was the finer and braver part. It was his fate to make a great many still more "prepared" people than me not inconsiderably wince; but there was no grain of bravado in his ripest things (I've always maintained it, though often contradicted), and at bottom the poor fellow, disinterested to his finger-tips and regarding imperfection not only as an aesthetic but quite also as a social crime, had an extreme dread of scandal. There are critics who regret that having gone so far he didn't go further; but I regret nothing--putting aside two or three of the motives I just mentioned-- since he arrived at a noble rarity and I don't see how you can go beyond that. The hours I spent in his study--this first one and the few that followed it; they were not, after all, so numerous--seem to glow, as I look back on them, with a tone that is partly that of the brown old room, rich, under the shaded candle-light where we sat and smoked, with the dusky deli-cate bindings of valuable books; partly that of his voice, of which I still catch the echo, charged with the fancies and figures that came at his command. When we went back to the drawing-room we found Miss Ambient alone in possession and prompt to mention that her sister-in-law had a quarter of an hour before been called by the nurse to see the child, who appeared rather unwell--a little feverish.

"Feverish! how in the world comes he to be feverish?" Ambient asked. "He was perfectly right this afternoon."

"Beatrice says you walked him about too much--you almost killed him."

"Beatrice must be very happy--she has an opportunity to triumph!" said my friend with a bright bitterness which was all I could have wished it.

"Surely not if the child's ill," I ventured to remark by way of plead-ing for Mrs. Ambient.

"My dear fellow, you aren't married--you don't know the nature of wives!" my host returned with spirit.

I tried to match it. "Possibly not; but I know the nature of mothers."

"Beatrice is perfect as a mother," sighed Miss Ambient quite tremendously and with her fingers interlaced on her embroidered knees.

"I shall go up and see my boy," her brother went on." Do you suppose he's asleep?"

"Beatrice won't let you see him, dear"--as to which our young lady looked at me, though addressing our companion.

"Do you call that being perfect as a mother?" Ambient asked.

"Yes, from her point of view."

"Damn her point of view!" cried the author of "Beltraffio." And he left the room; after which we heard him ascend the stairs.

I sat there for some ten minutes with Miss Ambient, and we naturally had some exchange of remarks, which began, I think, by my asking her what the point of view of her sister-in-law could be.

"Oh it's so very odd. But we're so very odd altogether. Don't you find us awfully unlike others of our class?--which indeed mostly, in England, is awful. We've lived so much abroad. I adore 'abroad.' Have you people like us in America?"

"You're not all alike, you interesting three--or, counting Dolcino, four--surely, surely; so that I don't think I understand your question. We've no one like your brother--I may go so far as that."

"You've probably more persons like his wife," Miss Ambient desolately smiled.

"I can tell you that better when you've told me about her point of view."

"Oh yes--oh yes. Well," said my entertainer, "she doesn't like his ideas. She doesn't like them for the child. She thinks them undesirable."

Being quite fresh from the contemplation of some of Mark Ambient's arcana I was particularly in a position to appreciate this announcement. But the effect of it was to make me, after staring a moment, burst into laughter which I instantly checked when I remembered the indisposed child above and the possibility of parents nervously or fussily anxious.

"What has that infant to do with ideas?" I asked. "Surely he can't tell one from another. Has he read his father's novels?"

"He's very precocious and very sensitive, and his mother thinks she can't begin to guard him too early." Miss Ambient's head drooped a little to one side and her eyes fixed themselves on futurity. Then of a sudden came a strange alteration; her face lighted to an effect more joyless than any gloom, to that indeed of a conscious insincere grimace, and she added "When one has children what one writes becomes a great responsibility."

"Children are terrible critics," I prosaically answered. "I'm really glad I haven't any."

"Do you also write, then? And in the same style as my brother? And do you like that style? And do people appreciate it in America? I don't write, but I think I feel." To these and various other inquiries and observations my young lady treated me till we heard her brother's step in the hall again and Mark Ambient reappeared. He was so flushed and grave that I supposed he had seen something symptomatic in the condition of his child. His sister apparently had another idea; she gazed at him from afar--as if he had been a burning ship on the horizon--and simply murmured "Poor old Mark!"

"I hope you're not anxious," I as promptly pronounced.

"No, but I'm disappointed. She won't let me in. She has locked the door, and I'm afraid to make a noise." I daresay there might have been a touch of the ridiculous in such a confession, but I liked my new friend so much that it took nothing for me from his dignity. "She tells me--from behind the door--that she'll let me know if he's worse."

"It's very good of her," said Miss Ambient with a hollow sound.

I had exchanged a glance with Mark in which it's possible he read that my pity for him was untinged with contempt, though I scarce know why he should have cared; and as his sister soon afterward got up and took her bedroom candlestick he proposed we should go back to his study. We sat there till after midnight; he put himself into his slippers and an old velvet jacket, he lighted an ancient pipe, but he talked considerably less than before. There were longish pauses in our communion, but they only made me feel we had advanced in intimacy. They helped me further to understand my friend's personal situation and to imagine it by no means the happiest possible. When his face was quiet it was vaguely troubled, showing, to my increase of interest--if that was all that was wanted!--that for him too life was the same struggle it had been for so many another man of genius. At last I prepared to leave him, and then, to my ineffable joy, he gave me some of the sheets of his forthcoming book--which, though unfinished, he had indulged in the luxury, so dear to writers of deliberation, of having "set up," from chapter to chapter, as he advanced. These early pages, the premices, in the language of letters, of that new fruit of his imagination, I should take to my room and look over at my leisure. I was in the act of leaving him when the door of the study noiselessly opened and Mrs. Ambient stood before us. She observed us a moment, her candle in her hand, and then said to her husband that as she supposed he hadn't gone to bed she had come down to let him know Dolcino was more quiet and would probably be better in the morning. Mark Ambient made no reply; he simply slipped past her in the doorway, as if for fear she might seize him in his passage, and bounded upstairs to judge for himself of his child's condition. She looked so frankly discomfited that I for a moment believed her about to give him chase. But she resigned herself with a sigh and her eyes turned, ruefully and without a ray, to the lamplit room where various books at which I had been looking were pulled out of their places on the shelves and the fumes of tobacco hung in mid-air. I bade her good-night and then, without intention, by a kind of fatality, a perversity that had already made me address her overmuch on that question of her husband's powers, I alluded to the precious proof-sheets with which Ambient had entrusted me and which I nursed there under my arm. "They're the opening chapters of his new book," I said. "Fancy my satisfaction at being allowed to carry them to my room!"

She turned away, leaving me to take my candlestick from the table in the hall; but before we separated, thinking it apparently a good occasion to let me know once for all since I was beginning, it would seem, to be quite "thick" with my host--that there was no fitness in my appealing to her for sympathy in such a case; before we separated, I say, she remarked to me with her quick fine well-bred inveterate curtness: "I daresay you attribute to me ideas I haven't got. I don't take that sort of interest in my husband's proof-sheets. I consider his writings most objectionable!"

CHAPTER III

I had an odd colloquy the next morning with Miss Ambient, whom I found strolling in the garden before breakfast. The whole place looked as fresh and trim, amid the twitter of the birds, as if, an hour before, the housemaids had been turned into it with their dust- pans and feather-brushes. I almost hesitated to light a cigarette and was doubly startled when, in the act of doing so, I suddenly saw the sister of my host, who had, at the best, something of the weirdness of an apparition, stand before me. She might have been posing for her photograph. Her sad-coloured robe arranged itself in serpentine folds at her feet; her hands locked themselves listlessly together in front; her chin rested on a cinque-cento ruff. The first thing I did after bidding her good-morning was to ask her for news of her little nephew--to express the hope she had heard he was better. She was able to gratify this trust--she spoke as if we might expect to see him during the day. We walked through the shrubberies together and she gave me further light on her brother's household, which offered me an opportunity to repeat to her what his wife had so startled and distressed me with the night before. WAS it the sorry truth that she thought his productions objectionable?

"She doesn't usually come out with that so soon!" Miss Ambient returned in answer to my breathlessness.

"Poor lady," I pleaded, "she saw I'm a fanatic."

"Yes, she won't like you for that. But you mustn't mind, if the rest of us like you! Beatrice thinks a work of art ought to have a 'purpose.' But she's a charming woman--don't you think her charming? I find in her quite the grand air."

"She's very beautiful," I produced with an effort; while I reflected that though it was apparently true that Mark Ambient was mismated it was also perceptible that his sister was perfidious. She assured me her brother and his wife had no other difference but this--one that she thought his writings immoral and his influence pernicious. It was a fixed idea; she was afraid of these things for the child. I answered that it was in all conscience enough, the trifle of a woman's regarding her husband's mind as a well of corruption, and she seemed much struck with the novelty of my remark. "But there hasn't been any of the sort of trouble that there so often is among married people," she said. "I suppose you can judge for yourself that Beatrice isn't at all--well, whatever they call it when a woman kicks over! And poor Mark doesn't make love to other people either. You might think he would, but I assure you he doesn't. All the same of course, from her point of view, you know, she has a dread of my brother's influence on the child on the formation of his character, his 'ideals,' poor little brat, his principles. It's as if it were a subtle poison or a contagion--something that would rub off on his tender sensibility when his father kisses him or holds him on his knee. If she could she'd prevent Mark from even so much as touching him. Every one knows it--visitors see it for themselves; so there's no harm in my telling you. Isn't it excessively odd? It comes from Beatrice's being so religious and so tremendously moral--so a cheval on fifty thousand riguardi. And then of course we mustn't forget," my companion added, a little unexpectedly, to this polyglot proposition, "that some of Mark's ideas are--well, really--rather impossible, don't you know?"

I reflected as we went into the house, where we found Ambient unfolding The Observer at the breakfast-table, that none of them were probably quite so "impossible, don't you know?" as his sister. Mrs. Ambient, a little "the worse," as was mentioned, for her ministrations, during the night, to Dolcino, didn't appear at breakfast. Her husband described her, however, as hoping to go to church. I afterwards learnt that she did go, but nothing naturally was less on the cards than that we should accompany her. It was while the church-bell droned near at hand that the author of "Beltraffio" led me forth for the ramble he had spoken of in his note. I shall attempt here no record of where we went or of what we saw. We kept to the fields and copses and commons, and breathed the same sweet air as the nibbling donkeys and the browsing sheep, whose woolliness seemed to me, in those early days of acquaintance with English objects, but part of the general texture of the small dense landscape, which looked as if the harvest were gathered by the shears and with all nature bleating and braying for the violence. Everything was full of expression for Mark Ambient's visitor--from the big bandy-legged geese whose whiteness was a "note" amid all the tones of green as they wandered beside a neat little oval pool, the foreground of a thatched and whitewashed inn, with a grassy approach and a pictorial sign--from these humble wayside animals to the crests of high woods which let a gable or a pinnacle peep here and there and looked even at a distance like trees of good company, conscious of an individual profile. I admired the hedge-rows, I plucked the faint- hued heather, and I was for ever stopping to say how charming I thought the thread-like footpaths across the fields, which wandered in a diagonal of finer grain from one smooth stile to another. Mark Ambient was abundantly good-natured and was as much struck, dear man, with some of my observations as I was with the literary allusions of the landscape. We sat and smoked on stiles, broaching paradoxes in the decent English air; we took short cuts across a park or two where the bracken was deep and my companion nodded to the old woman at the gate; we skirted rank coverts which rustled here and there as we passed, and we stretched ourselves at last on a heathery hillside where if the sun wasn't too hot neither was the earth too cold, and where the country lay beneath us in a rich blue mist. Of course I had already told him what I thought of his new novel, having the previous night read every word of the opening chapters before I went to bed.

"I'm not without hope of being able to make it decent enough," he said as I went back to the subject while we turned up our heels to the sky. "At least the people who dislike my stuff--and there are plenty of them, I believe--will dislike this thing (if it does turn out well) most." This was the first time I had heard him allude to the people who couldn't read him--a class so generally conceived to sit heavy on the consciousness of the man of letters. A being organised for literature as Mark Ambient was must certainly have had the normal proportion of sensitiveness, of irritability; the artistic ego, capable in some cases of such monstrous development, must have been in his composition sufficiently erect and active. I won't therefore go so far as to say that he never thought of his detractors or that he had any illusions with regard to the number of his admirers--he could never so far have deceived himself as to believe he was popular, but I at least then judged (and had occasion to be sure later on) that stupidity ruffled him visibly but little, that he had an air of thinking it quite natural he should leave many simple folk, tasting of him, as simple as ever he found them, and that he very seldom talked about the newspapers, which, by the way, were always even abnormally vulgar about him. Of course he may have thought them over--the newspapers--night and day; the only point I make is that he didn't show it while at the same time he didn't strike one as a man actively on his guard. I may add that, touching his hope of making the work on which he was then engaged the best of his books, it was only partly carried out. That place belongs incontestably to "Beltraffio," in spite of the beauty of certain parts of its successor. I quite believe, however, that he had at the moment of which I speak no sense of having declined; he was in love with his idea, which was indeed magnificent, and though for him, as I suppose for every sane artist, the act of execution had in it as much torment as joy, he saw his result grow like the crescent of the young moon and promise to fill the disk. "I want to be truer than I've ever been," he said, settling himself on his back with his hands clasped behind his head; "I want to give the impression of life itself. No, you may say what you will, I've always arranged things too much, always smoothed them down and rounded them off and tucked them in--done everything to them that life doesn't do. I've been a slave to the old superstitions."

"You a slave, my dear Mark Ambient? You've the freest imagination of our day!"

"All the more shame to me to have done some of the things I have! The reconciliation of the two women in 'Natalina,' for instance, which could never really have taken place. That sort of thing's ignoble--I blush when I think of it! This new affair must be a golden vessel, filled with the purest distillation of the actual; and oh how it worries me, the shaping of the vase, the hammering of the metal! I have to hammer it so fine, so smooth; I don't do more than an inch or two a day. And all the while I have to be so careful not to let a drop of the liquor escape! When I see the kind of things Life herself, the brazen hussy, does, I despair of ever catching her peculiar trick. She has an impudence, Life! If one risked a fiftieth part of the effects she risks! It takes ever so long to believe it. You don't know yet, my dear youth. It isn't till one has been watching her some forty years that one finds out half of what she's up to! Therefore one's earlier things must inevitably contain a mass of rot. And with what one sees, on one side, with its tongue in its cheek, defying one to be real enough, and on the other the bonnes gens rolling up their eyes at one's cynicism, the situation has elements of the ludicrous which the poor reproducer himself is doubtless in a position to appreciate better than any one else. Of course one mustn't worry about the bonnes gens," Mark Ambient went on while my thoughts reverted to his ladylike wife as interpreted by his remarkable sister.

"To sink your shaft deep and polish the plate through which people look into it--that's what your work consists of," I remember ingeniously observing.

"Ah polishing one's plate--that's the torment of execution!" he exclaimed, jerking himself up and sitting forward. "The effort to arrive at a surface, if you think anything of that decent sort necessary--some people don't, happily for them! My dear fellow, if you could see the surface I dream of as compared with the one with which I've to content myself. Life's really too short for art--one hasn't time to make one's shell ideally hard. Firm and bright, firm and bright is very well to say--the devilish thing has a way sometimes of being bright, and even of being hard, as mere tough frozen pudding is hard, without being firm. When I rap it with my knuckles it doesn't give the right sound. There are horrible sandy stretches where I've taken the wrong turn because I couldn't for the life of me find the right. If you knew what a dunce I am sometimes! Such things figure to me now base pimples and ulcers on the brow of beauty!"

"They're very bad, very bad," I said as gravely as I could.

"Very bad? They're the highest social offence I know; it ought--it absolutely ought; I'm quite serious--to be capital. If I knew I should be publicly thrashed else I'd manage to find the true word. The people who can't--some of them don't so much as know it when they see it-- would shut their inkstands, and we shouldn't be deluged by this flood of rubbish!"

I shall not attempt to repeat everything that passed between us, nor to explain just how it was that, every moment I spent in his company, Mark Ambient revealed to me more and more the consistency of his creative spirit, the spirit in him that felt all life as plastic material. I could but envy him the force of that passion, and it was at any rate through the receipt of this impression that by the time we returned I had gained the sense of intimacy with him that I have noted. Before we got up for the homeward stretch he alluded to his wife's having once-- or perhaps more than once--asked him whether he should like Dolcino to read "Beltraffio." He must have been unaware at the moment of all that this conveyed to me--as well doubtless of my extreme curiosity to hear what he had replied. He had said how much he hoped Dolcino would read ALL his works--when he was twenty; he should like him to know what his father had done. Before twenty it would be useless; he wouldn't understand them.

"And meanwhile do you propose to hide them--to lock them up in a drawer?" Mrs. Ambient had proceeded.

"Oh no--we must simply tell him they're not intended for small boys. If you bring him up properly after that he won't touch them."

To this Mrs. Ambient had made answer that it might be very awk- ward when he was about fifteen, say; and I asked her husband if it were his opinion in general, then, that young people shouldn't read novels.

"Good ones--certainly not!" said my companion. I suppose I had had other views, for I remember saying that for myself I wasn't sure it was bad for them if the novels were "good" to the right intensity of goodness. "Bad for THEM, I don't say so much!" my companion returned. "But very bad, I'm afraid, for the poor dear old novel itself." That oblique accidental allusion to his wife's attitude was followed by a greater breadth of reference as we walked home. "The difference between us is simply the opposition between two distinct ways of looking at the world, which have never succeeded in getting on together, or in making any kind of common household, since the beginning of time. They've borne all sorts of names, and my wife would tell you it's the difference between Christian and Pagan. I may be a pagan, but I don't like the name; it sounds sectarian. She thinks me at any rate no better than an ancient Greek. It's the difference between making the most of life and making the least, so that you'll get another better one in some other time and place. Will it be a sin to make the most of that one, too, I wonder; and shall we have to be bribed off in the future state as well as in the present? Perhaps I care too much for beauty--I don't know, I doubt if a poor devil CAN; I delight in it, I adore it, I think of it continually, I try to produce it, to reproduce it. My wife holds that we shouldn't cultivate or enjoy it without extraordinary precautions and reserves. She's always afraid of it, always on her guard. I don't know what it can ever have done to her, what grudge it owes her or what resentment rides. And she's so pretty, too, herself! Don't you think she's lovely? She was at any rate when we married. At that time I wasn't aware of that difference I speak of-- I thought it all came to the same thing: in the end, as they say. Well, perhaps it will in the end. I don't know what the end will be. Moreover, I care for seeing things as they are; that's the way I try to show them in any professed picture. But you mustn't talk to Mrs. Ambient about things as they are. She has a mortal dread of things as they are."

"She's afraid of them for Dolcino," I said: surprised a moment afterwards at being in a position--thanks to Miss Ambient--to be so explanatory; and surprised even now that Mark shouldn't have shown visibly that he wondered what the deuce I knew about it. But he didn't; he simply declared with a tenderness that touched me: "Ah nothing shall ever hurt HIM!"

He told me more about his wife before we arrived at the gate of home, and if he be judged to have aired overmuch his grievance I'm afraid I must admit that he had some of the foibles as well as the gifts of the artistic temperament; adding, however, instantly that hitherto, to the best of my belief, he had rarely let this particular cat out of the bag. "She thinks me immoral--that's the long and short of it," he said as we paused outside a moment and his hand rested on one of the bars of his gate; while his conscious expressive perceptive eyes--the eyes of a foreigner, I had begun to account them, much more than of the usual Englishman--viewing me now evidently as quite a familiar friend, took part in the declaration. "It's very strange when one thinks it all over, and there's a grand comicality in it that I should like to bring out. She's a very nice woman, extraordinarily well-behaved, upright and clever and with a tremendous lot of good sense about a good many matters. Yet her conception of a novel--she has explained it to me once or twice, and she doesn't do it badly as exposition--is a thing so false that it makes me blush. It's a thing so hollow, so dishonest, so lying, in which life is so blinked and blinded, so dodged and disfigured, that it makes my ears burn. It's two different ways of looking at the whole affair," he repeated, pushing open the gate. "And they're irreconcilable!" he added with a sigh. We went forward to the house, but on the walk, half-way to the door, he stopped and said to me: "If you're going into this kind of thing there's a fact you should know beforehand; it may save you some disappointment. There's a hatred of art, there's a hatred of literature--I mean of the genuine kinds. Oh the shams--those they'll swallow by the bucket!" I looked up at the charming house, with its genial colour and crookedness, and I answered with a smile that those evil passions might exist, but that I should never have expected to find them there. "Ah it doesn't matter after all," he a bit nervously laughed; which I was glad to hear, for I was reproaching myself with having worked him up.

If I had it soon passed off, for at luncheon he was delightful; strangely delightful considering that the difference between himself and his wife was, as he had said, irreconcilable. He had the art, by his manner, by his smile, by his natural amenity, of reducing the importance of it in the common concerns of life; and Mrs. Ambient, I must add, lent herself to this transaction with a very good grace. I watched her at table for further illustrations of that fixed idea of which Miss Ambient had spoken to me; for in the light of the united revelations of her sister-in-law and her husband she had come to seem to me almost a sinister personage. Yet the signs of a sombre fanaticism were not more immediately striking in her than before; it was only after a while that her air of incorruptible conformity, her tapering monosyllabic correctness, began to affect me as in themselves a cold thin flame. Certainly, at first, she resembled a woman with as few passions as possible; but if she had a passion at all it would indeed be that of Philistinism. She might have been (for there are guardian-spirits, I suppose, of all great principles) the very angel of the pink of propriety--putting the pink for a principle, though I'd rather put some dismal cold blue. Mark Ambient, apparently, ten years before, had simply and quite inevitably taken her for an angel, without asking himself of what. He had been right in calling my attention to her beauty. In looking for some explanation of his original surrender to her I saw more than before that she was, physically speaking, a wonderfully cultivated human plant--that he might well have owed her a brief poetic inspiration. It was impossible to be more propped and pencilled, more delicately tinted and petalled.

If I had had it in my heart to think my host a little of a hypocrite for appearing to forget at table everything he had said to me in our walk, I should instantly have cancelled such a judgement on reflecting that the good news his wife was able to give him about their little boy was ground enough for any optimistic reaction. It may have come partly, too, from a certain compunction at having breathed to me at all harshly on the cool fair lady who sat there--a desire to prove himself not after all so mismated. Dolcino continued to be much better, and it had been promised him he should come downstairs after his dinner. As soon as we had risen from our own meal Mark slipped away, evidently for the purpose of going to his child; and no sooner had I observed this than I became aware his wife had simultaneously vanished. It happened that Miss Ambient and I, both at the same moment, saw the tail of her dress whisk out of a doorway; an incident that led the young lady to smile at me as if I now knew all the secrets of the Ambients. I passed with her into the garden and we sat down on a dear old bench that rested against the west wall of the house. It was a perfect spot for the middle period of a Sunday in June, and its felicity seemed to come partly from an antique sun-dial which, rising in front of us and forming the centre of a small intricate parterre, measured the moments ever so slowly and made them safe for leisure and talk. The garden bloomed in the suffused afternoon, the tall beeches stood still for an example, and, behind and above us, a rose tree of many seasons, clinging to the faded grain of the brick, expressed the whole character of the scene in a familiar exquisite smell. It struck me as a place to offer genius every favour and sanction--not to bristle with challenges and checks. Miss Ambient asked me if I had enjoyed my walk with her brother and whether we had talked of many things.

"Well, of most things," I freely allowed, though I remembered we hadn't talked of Miss Ambient.

"And don't you think some of his theories are very peculiar?"

"Oh I guess I agree with them all." I was very particular, for Miss Ambient's entertainment, to guess.

"Do you think art's everything?" she put to me in a moment.

"In art, of course I do!"

"And do you think beauty's everything?"

"Everything's a big word, which I think we should use as little as possible. But how can we not want beauty?"

"Ah there you are!" she sighed, though I didn't quite know what she meant by it. "Of course it's difficult for a woman to judge how far to go," she went on. "I adore everything that gives a charm to life. I'm intensely sensitive to form. But sometimes I draw back--don't you see what I mean?--I don't quite see where I shall be landed. I only want to be quiet, after all," Miss Ambient continued as if she had long been baffled of this modest desire. "And one must be good, at any rate, must not one?" she pursued with a dubious quaver--an intimation apparently that what I might say one way or the other would settle it for her. It was difficult for me to be very original in reply, and I'm afraid I repaid her confidence with an unblushing platitude. I remember, moreover, attaching to it an inquiry, equally destitute of freshness and still more wanting perhaps in tact, as to whether she didn't mean to go to church, since that was an obvious way of being good. She made answer that she had performed this duty in the morning, and that for her, of Sunday afternoons, supreme virtue consisted in answering the week's letters. Then suddenly and without transition she brought out: "It's quite a mistake about Dolcino's being better. I've seen him and he's not at all right."

I wondered, and somehow I think I scarcely believed. "Surely his mother would know, wouldn't she?"

She appeared for a moment to be counting the leaves on one of the great beeches. "As regards most matters one can easily say what, in a given situation, my sister-in-law will, or would, do. But in the present case there are strange elements at work."

"Strange elements? Do you mean in the constitution of the child?"

"No, I mean in my sister-in-law's feelings."

"Elements of affection of course; elements of anxiety," I concurred. "But why do you call them strange?"

She repeated my words. "Elements of affection, elements of anxiety. She's very anxious."

Miss Ambient put me indescribably ill at ease; she almost scared me, and I wished she would go and write her letters. "His father will have seen him now," I said, "and if he's not satisfied he will send for the doctor."

"The doctor ought to have been here this morning," she promptly returned. "He lives only two miles away."

I reflected that all this was very possibly but a part of the general tragedy of Miss Ambient's view of things; yet I asked her why she hadn't urged that view on her sister-in-law. She answered me with a smile of extraordinary significance and observed that I must have very little idea of her "peculiar" relations with Beatrice; but I must do her the justice that she re-enforced this a little by the plea that any distinguishable alarm of Mark's was ground enough for a difference of his wife's. He was always nervous about the child, and as they were predestined by nature to take opposite views, the only thing for the mother was to cultivate a false optimism. In Mark's absence and that of his betrayed fear she would have been less easy. I remembered what he had said to me about their dealings with their son--that between them they'd probably put an end to him; but I didn't repeat this to Miss Ambient: the less so that just then her brother emerged from the house, carrying the boy in his arms. Close behind him moved his wife, grave and pale; the little sick face was turned over Ambient's shoulder and toward the mother. We rose to receive the group, and as they came near us Dolcino twisted himself about. His enchanting eyes showed me a smile of recognition, in which, for the moment, I should have taken a due degree of comfort. Miss Ambient, however, received another impression, and I make haste to say that her quick sensibility, which visibly went out to the child, argues that in spite of her affectations she might have been of some human use. "It won't do at all--it won't do at all," she said to me under her breath. "I shall speak to Mark about the Doctor."

Her small nephew was rather white, but the main difference I saw in him was that he was even more beautiful than the day before. He had been dressed in his festal garments--a velvet suit and a crimson sash--and he looked like a little invalid prince too young to know condescension and smiling familiarly on his subjects.

"Put him down, Mark, he's not a bit at his ease," Mrs. Ambient said.

"Should you like to stand on your feet, my boy?" his father asked.

He made a motion that quickly responded. "Oh yes; I'm remarkably well."

Mark placed him on the ground; he had shining pointed shoes with enormous bows. "Are you happy now, Mr. Ambient?"

"Oh yes, I'm particularly happy," Dolcino replied. But the words were scarce out of his mouth when his mother caught him up and, in a moment, holding him on her knees, took her place on the bench where Miss Ambient and I had been sitting. This young lady said something to her brother, in consequence of which the two wandered away into the garden together.

CHAPTER IV

I remained with Mrs. Ambient, but as a servant had brought out a couple of chairs I wasn't obliged to seat myself beside her. Our conversation failed of ease, and I, for my part, felt there would be a shade of hypocrisy in my now trying to make myself agreeable to the partner of my friend's existence. I didn't dislike her--I rather admired her; but I was aware that I differed from her inexpressibly. Then I suspected, what I afterwards definitely knew and have already intimated, that the poor lady felt small taste for her husband's so undisguised disciple; and this of course was not encouraging. She thought me an obtrusive and designing, even perhaps a depraved, young man whom a perverse Providence had dropped upon their quiet lawn to flatter his worst tendencies. She did me the honour to say to Miss Ambient, who repeated the speech, that she didn't know when she had seen their companion take such a fancy to a visitor; and she measured apparently my evil influence by Mark's appreciation of my society. I had a consciousness, not oppressive but quite sufficient, of all this; though I must say that if it chilled my flow of small-talk it yet didn't prevent my thinking the beautiful mother and beautiful child, interlaced there against their background of roses, a picture such as I doubtless shouldn't soon see again. I was free, I supposed, to go into the house and write letters, to sit in the drawing-room, to repair to my own apartment and take a nap;

but the only use I made of my freedom was to linger still in my chair and say to myself that the light hand of Sir Joshua might have painted Mark Ambient's wife and son. I found myself looking perpetually at the latter small mortal, who looked constantly back at me, and that was enough to detain me. With these vaguely-amused eyes he smiled, and I felt it an absolute impossibility to abandon a child with such an expression. His attention never strayed; it attached itself to my face as if among all the small incipient things of his nature throbbed a desire to say something to me. If I could have taken him on my own knee he perhaps would have managed to say it; but it would have been a critical matter to ask his mother to give him up, and it has remained a constant regret for me that on that strange Sunday afternoon I didn't even for a moment hold Dolcino in my arms. He had said he felt remarkably well and was especially happy; but though peace may have been with him as he pillowed his charming head on his mother's breast, dropping his little crimson silk legs from her lap, I somehow didn't think security was. He made no attempt to walk about; he was content to swing his legs softly and strike one as languid and angelic.

Mark returned to us with his sister; and Miss Ambient, repeating her mention of the claims of her correspondence, passed into the house. Mark came and stood in front of his wife, looking down at the child, who immediately took hold of his hand and kept it while he stayed. "I think Mackintosh ought to see him," he said; "I think I'll walk over and fetch him."

"That's Gwendolen's idea, I suppose," Mrs. Ambient replied very sweetly.

"It's not such an out-of-the-way idea when one's child's ill," he returned.

"I'm not ill, papa; I'm much better now," sounded in the boy's silver pipe.

"Is that the truth, or are you only saying it to be agreeable? You've a great idea of being agreeable, you know."

The child seemed to meditate on this distinction, this imputation, for a moment; then his exaggerated eyes, which had wandered, caught my own as I watched him. "Do YOU think me agreeable?" he inquired with the candour of his age and with a look that made his father turn round to me laughing and ask, without saying it, "Isn't he adorable?"

"Then why don't you hop about, if you feel so lusty?" Ambient went on while his son swung his hand.

"Because mamma's holding me close!"

"Oh yes; I know how mamma holds you when I come near!" cried Mark with a grimace at his wife.

She turned her charming eyes up to him without deprecation or concession. "You can go for Mackintosh if you like. I think myself it would be better. You ought to drive."

"She says that to get me away," he put to me with a gaiety that I thought a little false; after which he started for the Doctor's.

I remained there with Mrs. Ambient, though even our exchange of twaddle had run very thin. The boy's little fixed white face seemed, as before, to plead with me to stay, and after a while it produced still another effect, a very curious one, which I shall find it difficult to express. Of course I expose myself to the charge of an attempt to justify by a strained logic after the fact a step which may have been on my part but the fruit of a native want of discretion; and indeed the traceable consequences of that perversity were too lamentable to leave me any desire to trifle with the question. All I can say is that I acted in perfect good faith and that Dolcino's friendly little gaze gradually kindled the spark of my inspiration. What helped it to glow were the other influences--

the silent suggestive garden-nook, the perfect opportunity (if it was not an opportunity for that it was an opportunity for nothing) and the plea I speak of, which issued from the child's eyes and seemed to make him say: "The mother who bore me and who presses me here to her bosom--sympathetic little organism that I am--has really the kind of sensibility she has been represented to you as lacking, if you only look for it patiently and respectfully. How is it conceivable she shouldn't have it? How is it possible that *I* should have so much of it--for I'm quite full of it, dear strange gentleman--if it weren't also in some degree in her? I'm my great father's child, but I'm also my beautiful mother's, and I'm sorry for the difference between them!" So it shaped itself before me, the vision of reconciling Mrs. Ambient with her husband, of putting an end to their ugly difference. The project was absurd of course, for had I not had his word for it--spoken with all the bitterness of experience--that the gulf dividing them was well-nigh bottomless? Nevertheless, a quarter of an hour after Mark had left us, I observed to my hostess that I couldn't get over what she had told me the night before about her thinking her husband's compositions "objectionable." I had been so very sorry to hear it, had thought of it constantly and wondered whether it mightn't be possible to make her change her mind. She gave me a great cold stare, meant apparently as an admonition to me to mind my business. I wish I had taken this mute counsel, but I didn't take it. I went on to remark that it seemed an immense pity so much that was interesting should be lost on her.

"Nothing's lost upon me," she said in a tone that didn't make the contradiction less. "I know they're very interesting."

"Don't you like papa's books?" Dolcino asked, addressing his mother but still looking at me. Then he added to me: "Won't you read them to me, American gentleman?"

"I'd rather tell you some stories of my own," I said. "I know some that are awfully good."

"When will you tell them? To-morrow?"

"To-morrow with pleasure, if that suits you."

His mother took this in silence. Her husband, during our walk, had asked me to remain another day; my promise to her son was an implication that I had consented, and it wasn't possible the news could please her. This ought doubtless to have made me more careful as to what I said next, but all I can plead is that it didn't. I soon mentioned that just after leaving her the evening before, and after hearing her apply to her husband's writings the epithet already quoted, I had on going up to my room sat down to the perusal of those sheets of his new book that he had been so good as to lend me. I had sat entranced till nearly three in the morning--I had read them twice over. "You say you haven't looked at them. I think it's such a pity you shouldn't. Do let me beg you to take them up. They're so very remarkable. I'm sure they'll convert you. They place him in-- really--such a dazzling light. All that's best in him is there. I've no doubt it's a great liberty, my saying all this; but pardon me, and DO read them!"

"Do read them, mamma!" the boy again sweetly shrilled. "Do read them!"

She bent her head and closed his lips with a kiss. "Of course I know he has worked immensely over them," she said; after which she made no remark, but attached her eyes thoughtfully to the ground. The tone of these last words was such as to leave me no spirit for further pressure, and after hinting at a fear that her husband mightn't have caught the Doctor I got up and took a turn about the grounds. When I came back ten minutes later she was still in her place watching her boy, who had fallen asleep in her lap. As I drew near she put her finger to her lips and a short time afterwards rose, holding him; it being now best, she said, that she should take him upstairs. I offered to carry him and opened my arms for the purpose; but she thanked me and turned away with the child still in her embrace, his head on her shoulder. "I'm very strong," was her last word as she passed into the house, her slim flexible figure bent backward with the filial weight. So I never laid a longing hand on Dolcino.

I betook myself to Ambient's study, delighted to have a quiet hour to look over his books by myself. The windows were open to the garden; the sunny stillness, the mild light of the English summer, filled the room without quite chasing away the rich dusky tone that was a part of its charm and that abode in the serried shelves where old morocco exhaled the fragrance of curious learning, as well as in the brighter intervals where prints and medals and miniatures were suspended on a surface of faded stuff. The place had both colour and quiet; I thought it a perfect room for work and went so far as to say to myself that, if it were mine to sit and scribble in, there was no knowing but I might learn to write as well as the author of "Beltraffio." This distinguished man still didn't reappear, and I rummaged freely among his treasures. At last I took down a book that detained me a while and seated myself in a fine old leather chair by the window to turn it over. I had been occupied in this way for half an hour--a good part of the afternoon had waned--when I became conscious of another presence in the room and, looking up from my quarto, saw that Mrs. Ambient, having pushed open the door quite again in the same noiseless way marking or disguising her entrance the night before, had advanced across the threshold. On seeing me she stopped; she had not, I think, expected to find me. But her hesitation was only of a moment; she came straight to her husband's writing-table as if she were looking for something. I got up and asked her if I could help her. She glanced about an instant and then put her hand upon a roll of papers which I recognised, as I had placed it on that spot at the early hour of my descent from my room.

"Is this the new book?" she asked, holding it up.

"The very sheets," I smiled; "with precious annotations."

"I mean to take your advice"--and she tucked the little bundle under her arm. I congratulated her cordially and ventured to make of my triumph, as I presumed to call it, a subject of pleasantry. But she was perfectly grave and turned away from me, as she had presented herself, without relaxing her rigour; after which I settled down to my quarto again with the reflexion that Mrs. Ambient was truly an eccentric. My triumph, too, suddenly seemed to me rather vain. A woman who couldn't unbend at a moment exquisitely indicated would never understand Mark Ambient. He came back to us at last in person, having brought the Doctor with him. "He was away from home," Mark said, "and I went after him to where he was supposed to be. He had left the place, and I followed him to two or three others, which accounts for my delay." He was now with Mrs. Ambient, looking at the child, and was to see Mark again before leaving the house. My host noticed at the end of two minutes that the proof-sheets of his new book had been removed from the table; and when I told him, in reply to his question as to what I knew about them, that Mrs. Ambient had carried them off to read he turned almost pale with surprise. "What has suddenly made her so curious?" he cried; and I was obliged to tell him that I was at the bottom of the mystery. I had had it on my conscience to assure her that she really ought to know of what her husband was capable. "Of what I'm capable? Elle ne s'en doute que trop!" said Ambient with a laugh; but he took my meddling very good- naturedly and contented himself with adding that he was really much afraid she would burn up the sheets, his emendations and all, of which latter he had no duplicate. The Doctor paid a long visit in the nursery, and before he came down I retired to my own quarters, where I remained till dinner-time. On entering the drawing-room at this hour I found Miss Ambient in possession, as she had been the evening before.

"I was right about Dolcino," she said, as soon as she saw me, with an air of triumph that struck me as the climax of perversity. "He's really very ill."

"Very ill! Why when I last saw him, at four o'clock, he was in fairly good form."

"There has been a change for the worse, very sudden and rapid, and when the Doctor got here he found diphtheritic symptoms. He ought to have been called, as I knew, in the morning, and the child oughtn't to have been brought into the garden."

"My dear lady, he was very happy there," I protested with horror.

"He would be very happy anywhere. I've no doubt he's very happy now, with his poor little temperature--!" She dropped her voice as her brother came in, and Mark let us know that as a matter of course Mrs. Ambient wouldn't appear. It was true the boy had developed diphtheritic symptoms, but he was quiet for the present and his mother earnestly watching him. She was a perfect nurse, Mark said, and Mackintosh would come back at ten. Our dinner wasn't very gay-- with my host worried and absent; and his sister annoyed me by her constant tacit assumption, conveyed in the very way she nibbled her bread and sipped her wine, of having "told me so." I had had no disposition to deny anything she might have told me, and I couldn't see that her satisfaction in being justified by the event relieved her little nephew's condition. The truth is that, as the sequel was to prove, Miss Ambient had some of the qualities of the sibyl and had therefore perhaps a right to the sibylline contortions. Her brother was so preoccupied that I felt my presence an indiscretion and was sorry I had promised to remain over the morrow. I put it to Mark that clearly I had best leave them in the morning; to which he replied that, on the contrary, if he was to pass the next days in the fidgets my company would distract his attention. The fidgets had already begun for him, poor fellow; and as we sat in his study with our cigars after dinner he wandered to the door whenever he heard the sound of the Doctor's wheels. Miss Ambient, who shared this apartment with us, gave me at such moments significant glances; she had before rejoining us gone upstairs to ask about the child. His mother and his nurse gave a fair report, but Miss Ambient found his fever high and his symptoms very grave. The Doctor came at ten o'clock, and I went to bed after hearing from Mark that he saw no present cause for alarm. He had made every provision for the night and was to return early in the morning.

I quitted my room as eight struck the next day and when I came downstairs saw, through the open door of the house, Mrs. Ambient standing at the front gate of the grounds in colloquy with Mackintosh. She wore a white dressing-gown, but her shining hair was carefully tucked away in its net, and in the morning freshness, after a night of watching, she looked as much "the type of the lady" as her sister-in-law had described her. Her appearance, I suppose, ought to have reassured me; but I was still nervous and uneasy, so that I shrank from meeting her with the necessary challenge. None the less, however, was I impatient to learn how the new day found him; and as Mrs. Ambient hadn't seen me I passed into the grounds by a roundabout way and, stopping at a further gate, hailed the Doctor just as he was driving off. Mrs. Ambient had returned to the house before he got into his cart.

"Pardon me, but as a friend of the family I should like very much to hear about the little boy."

The stout sharp circumspect man looked at me from head to foot and then said: "I'm sorry to say I haven't seen him."

"Haven't seen him?"

"Mrs. Ambient came down to meet me as I alighted, and told me he was sleeping so soundly, after a restless night, that she didn't wish him disturbed. I assured her I wouldn't disturb him, but she said he was quite safe now and she could look after him herself."

"Thank you very much. Are you coming back?"

"No, sir; I'll be hanged if I come back!" cried the honest practitioner in high resentment. And the horse started as he settled beside his man.

I wandered back into the garden, and five minutes later Miss Ambient came forth from the house to greet me. She explained that breakfast wouldn't be served for some time and that she desired a moment herself with the Doctor. I let her know that the good vexed man had come and departed, and I repeated to her what he had told me about his dismissal. This made Miss Ambient very serious, very serious indeed, and she sank into a bench, with dilated eyes, hugging her elbows with crossed arms. She indulged in many strange signs, she confessed herself immensely distressed, and she finally told me what her own last news of her nephew had been. She had sat up very late-- after me, after Mark--and before going to bed had knocked at the door of the child's room, opened to her by the nurse. This good woman had admitted her and she had found him quiet, but flushed and "unnatural," with his mother sitting by his bed. "She held his hand in one of hers," said Miss Ambient, "and in the other--what do you think?--the proof-sheets of Mark's new book!" She was reading them there intently: "did you ever hear of anything so extraordinary? Such a very odd time to be reading an author whom she never could abide!" In her agitation Miss Ambient was guilty of this vulgarism of speech, and I was so impressed by her narrative that only in recalling her words later did I notice the lapse. Mrs. Ambient had looked up from her reading with her finger on her lips--I recognised the gesture she had addressed me in the afternoon-- and, though the nurse was about to go to rest, had not encouraged her sister-in-law to relieve her of any part of her vigil. But certainly at that time the boy's state was far from reassuring--his poor little breathing so painful; and what change could have taken place in him in those few hours that would justify Beatrice in denying Mackintosh access? This was the moral of Miss Ambient's anecdote, the moral for herself at least. The moral for me, rather, was that it WAS a very singular time for Mrs. Ambient to be going into a novelist she had never appreciated and who had simply happened to be recommended to her by a young American she disliked. I thought of her sitting there in the sick-chamber in the still hours of the night and after the nurse had left her, turning and turning those pages of genius and wrestling with their magical influence.

I must be sparing of the minor facts and the later emotions of this sojourn--it lasted but a few hours longer--and devote but three words to my subsequent relations with Ambient. They lasted five years-- till his death--and were full of interest, of satisfaction and, I may add, of sadness. The main thing to be said of these years is that I had a secret from him which I guarded to the end. I believe he never suspected it, though of this I'm not absolutely sure. If he had so much as an inkling the line he had taken, the line of absolute negation of the matter to himself, shows an immense effort of the will. I may at last lay bare my secret, giving it for what it is worth; now that the main sufferer has gone, that he has begun to be alluded to as one of the famous early dead and that his wife has ceased to survive him; now, too, that Miss Ambient, whom I also saw at intervals during the time that followed, has, with her embroideries and her attitudes, her necromantic glances and strange intuitions, retired to a Sisterhood, where, as I am told, she is deeply immured and quite lost to the world.

Mark came in to breakfast after this lady and I had for some time been seated there. He shook hands with me in silence, kissed my companion, opened his letters and newspapers and pretended to drink his coffee. But I took these movements for mechanical and was little surprised when he suddenly pushed away everything that was before him and, with his head in his hands and his elbows on the table, sat staring strangely at the cloth.

"What's the matter, caro fratello mio?" Miss Ambient quavered, peeping from behind the urn.

He answered nothing, but got up with a certain violence and strode to the window. We rose to our feet, his relative and I, by a common impulse, exchanging a glance of some alarm; and he continued to stare into the garden. "In heaven's name what has got possession of Beatrice?" he cried at last, turning round on us a ravaged face. He looked from one of us to the other--the appeal was addressed to us alike.

Miss Ambient gave a shrug. "My poor Mark, Beatrice is always--Beatrice!"

"She has locked herself up with the boy--bolted and barred the door. She refuses to let me come near him!" he went on.

"She refused to let Mackintosh see him an hour ago!" Miss Ambient promptly returned.

"Refused to let Mackintosh see him? By heaven I'll smash in the door!" And Mark brought his fist down upon the sideboard, which he had now approached, so that all the breakfast-service rang.

I begged Miss Ambient to go up and try to have speech of her sister-in-law, and I drew Mark out into the garden. "You're exceedingly nervous, and Mrs. Ambient's probably right," I there undertook to plead. "Women know; women should be supreme in such a situation. Trust a mother--a devoted mother, my dear friend!" With such words as these I tried to soothe and comfort him, and, marvellous to relate, I succeeded, with the help of many cigarettes, in making him walk about the garden and talk, or suffer me at least to do so, for near an hour. When about that time had elapsed his sister reappeared, reaching us rapidly and with a convulsed face while she held her hand to her heart.

"Go for the Doctor, Mark--go for the Doctor this moment!"

"Is he dying? Has she killed him?" my poor friend cried, flinging away his cigarette.

"I don't know what she has done! But she's frightened, and now she wants the Doctor."

"He told me he'd be hanged if he came back!" I felt myself obliged to mention.

"Precisely--therefore Mark himself must go for him, and not a messenger. You must see him and tell him it's to save your child. The trap has been ordered--it's ready."

"To save him? I'll save him, please God!" Ambient cried, bounding with his great strides across the lawn.

As soon as he had gone I felt I ought to have volunteered in his place, and I said as much to Miss Ambient; but she checked me by grasping my arm while we heard the wheels of the dog-cart rattle away from the gate. "He's off--he's off--and now I can think! To get him away--while I think--while I think!"

"While you think of what, Miss Ambient?"

"Of the unspeakable thing that has happened under this roof!"

Her manner was habitually that of such a prophetess of ill that I at first allowed for some great extravagance. But I looked at her hard, and the next thing felt myself turn white. "Dolcino IS dying then-- he's dead?"

"It's too late to save him. His mother has let him die! I tell you that because you're sympathetic, because you've imagination," Miss Ambient was good enough to add, interrupting my expression of horror. "That's why you had the idea of making her read Mark's new book!"

"What has that to do with it? I don't understand you. Your accusation's monstrous."

"I see it all--I'm not stupid," she went on, heedless of my emphasis. "It was the book that finished her--it was that decided her!"

"Decided her? Do you mean she has murdered her child?" I demanded, trembling at my own words.

"She sacrificed him; she determined to do nothing to make him live. Why else did she lock herself in, why else did she turn away the Doctor? The book gave her a horror; she determined to rescue him--to prevent him from ever being touched. He had a crisis at two o'clock in the morning. I know that from the nurse, who had left her then, but whom, for a short time, she called back. The darling got munch worse, but she insisted on the nurse's going back to bed, and after that she was alone with him for hours."

I listened with a dread that stayed my credence, while she stood there with her tearless glare. "Do you pretend then she has no pity, that she's cruel and insane?"

"She held him in her arms, she pressed him to her breast, not to see him; but she gave him no remedies; she did nothing the Doctor ordered. Everything's there untouched. She has had the honesty not even to throw the drugs away!"

I dropped upon the nearest bench, overcome with my dismay--quite as much at Miss Ambient's horrible insistence and distinctness as at the monstrous meaning of her words. Yet they came amazingly straight, and if they did have a sense I saw myself too woefully figure in it. Had I been then a proximate cause-- ? "You're a very strange woman and you say incredible things," I could only reply.

She had one of her tragic headshakes. "You think it necessary to protest, but you're really quite ready to believe me. You've received an impression of my sister-in-law--you've guessed of what she's capable."

I don't feel bound to say what concession on this score I made to Miss Ambient, who went on to relate to me that within the last half-hour Beatrice had had a revulsion, that she was tremendously frightened at what she had done; that her fright itself betrayed her; and that she would now give heaven and earth to save the child. "Let us hope she will!" I said, looking at my watch and trying to time poor Ambient; whereupon my companion repeated all portentously

"Let us hope so!" When I asked her if she herself could do nothing, and whether she oughtn't to be with her sister-in-law, she replied: "You had better go and judge! She's like a wounded tigress!"

I never saw Mrs. Ambient till six months after this, and therefore can't pretend to have verified the comparison. At the latter period she was again the type of the perfect lady. "She'll treat him better after this," I remember her sister-in-law's saying in response to some quick outburst, on my part, of compassion for her brother. Though I had been in the house but thirty-six hours this young lady had treated me with extraordinary confidence, and there was therefore a certain demand I might, as such an intimate, make of her. I extracted from her a pledge that she'd never say to her brother what she had just said to me, that she'd let him form his own theory of his wife's conduct. She agreed

with me that there was misery enough in the house without her con-
tributing a new anguish, and that Mrs. Ambient's proceedings might
be explained, to her husband's mind, by the extravagance of a jealous
devotion. Poor Mark came back with the Doctor much sooner than we
could have hoped, but we knew five minutes afterwards that it was all
too late. His sole, his adored little son was more exquisitely beautiful in
death than he had been in life. Mrs. Ambient's grief was frantic; she lost
her head and said strange things. As for Mark's--but I won't speak of
that. Basta, basta, as he used to say. Miss Ambient kept her secret--I've
already had occasion to say that she had her good points--but it rankled
in her conscience like a guilty participation and, I imagine, had something to do with her ultimately retiring from the world. And, apropos
of consciences, the reader is now in a position to judge of my compunction for my effort to convert my cold hostess. I ought to mention that
the death of her child in some degree converted her. When the new
book came out (it was long delayed) she read it over as a whole, and her
husband told me that during the few supreme weeks before her death-
-she failed rapidly after losing her son, sank into a consumption and
faded away at Mentone--she even dipped into the black "Beltraffio."

The Codes Of Hammurabi And Moses
W. W. Davies

QTY

The discovery of the Hammurabi Code is one of the greatest achievements of archaeology, and is of paramount interest, not only to the student of the Bible, but also to all those interested in ancient history...

Religion   **ISBN:** *1-59462-338-4*   **Pages:132**

MSRP $12.95

The Theory of Moral Sentiments
Adam Smith

QTY

This work from 1749. contains original theories of conscience amd moral judgment and it is the foundation for systemof morals.

Philosophy **ISBN:** *1-59462-777-0*   **Pages:536**

MSRP $19.95

Jessica's First Prayer
Hesba Stretton

QTY

In a screened and secluded corner of one of the many railway-bridges which span the streets of London there could be seen a few years ago, from five o'clock every morning until half past eight, a tidily set-out coffee-stall, consisting of a trestle and board, upon which stood two large tin cans, with a small fire of charcoal burning under each so as to keep the coffee boiling during the early hours of the morning when the work-people were thronging into the city on their way to their daily toil...

Pages:84

Childrens   **ISBN:** *1-59462-373-2*   *MSRP $9.95*

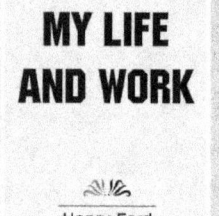

My Life and Work
Henry Ford

QTY

Henry Ford revolutionized the world with his implementation of mass production for the Model T automobile. Gain valuable business insight into his life and work with his own auto-biography... "We have only started on our development of our country we have not as yet, with all our talk of wonderful progress, done more than scratch the surface. The progress has been wonderful enough but..."

Pages:300

Biographies/   **ISBN:** *1-59462-198-5*   *MSRP $21.95*

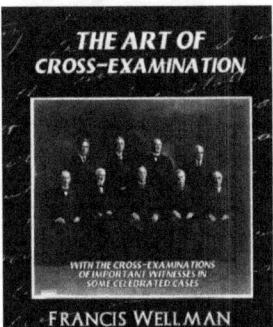

The Art of Cross-Examination
Francis Wellman

QTY

I presume it is the experience of every author, after his first book is published upon an important subject, to be almost overwhelmed with a wealth of ideas and illustrations which could readily have been included in his book, and which to his own mind, at least, seem to make a second edition inevitable. Such certainly was the case with me; and when the first edition had reached its sixth impression in five months, I rejoiced to learn that it seemed to my publishers that the book had met with a sufficiently favorable reception to justify a second and considerably enlarged edition. ..

Pages:412

Reference   ISBN: *1-59462-647-2*   *MSRP $19.95*

On the Duty of Civil Disobedience
Henry David Thoreau

QTY

Thoreau wrote his famous essay, On the Duty of Civil Disobedience, as a protest against an unjust but popular war and the immoral but popular institution of slave-owning. He did more than write—he declined to pay his taxes, and was hauled off to gaol in consequence. Who can say how much this refusal of his hastened the end of the war and of slavery ?

Law   ISBN: *1-59462-747-9*   **Pages:48**

MSRP $7.45

Dream Psychology Psychoanalysis for Beginners
Sigmund Freud

QTY

Sigmund Freud, born Sigismund Schlomo Freud (May 6, 1856 - September 23, 1939), was a Jewish-Austrian neurologist and psychiatrist who co-founded the psychoanalytic school of psychology. Freud is best known for his theories of the unconscious mind, especially involving the mechanism of repression; his redefinition of sexual desire as mobile and directed towards a wide variety of objects; and his therapeutic techniques, especially his understanding of transference in the therapeutic relationship and the presumed value of dreams as sources of insight into unconscious desires.

Pages:196

Psychology   ISBN: *1-59462-905-6*   *MSRP $15.45*

The Miracle of Right Thought
Orison Swett Marden

QTY

Believe with all of your heart that you will do what you were made to do. When the mind has once formed the habit of holding cheerful, happy, prosperous pictures, it will not be easy to form the opposite habit. It does not matter how improbable or how far away this realization may see, or how dark the prospects may be, if we visualize them as best we can, as vividly as possible, hold tenaciously to them and vigorously struggle to attain them, they will gradually become actualized, realized in the life. But a desire, a longing without endeavor, a yearning abandoned or held indifferently will vanish without realization.

Pages:360

Self Help   ISBN: *1-59462-644-8*   *MSRP $25.45*

QTY

The Rosicrucian Cosmo-Conception Mystic Christianity *by Max Heindel*   ISBN: *1-59462-188-8*   **$38.95**
The Rosicrucian Cosmo-conception is not dogmatic, neither does it appeal to any other authority than the reason of the student. It is: not controversial, but is: sent forth in the, hope that it may help to clear...   New Age/Religion Pages 646

Abandonment To Divine Providence *by Jean-Pierre de Caussade*   ISBN: *1-59462-228-0*   **$25.95**
"The Rev. Jean Pierre de Caussade was one of the most remarkable spiritual writers of the Society of Jesus in France in the 18th Century. His death took place at Toulouse in 1751. His works have gone through many editions and have been republished...   Inspirational/Religion Pages 400

Mental Chemistry *by Charles Haanel*   ISBN: *1-59462-192-6*   **$23.95**
Mental Chemistry allows the change of material conditions by combining and appropriately utilizing the power of the mind. Much like applied chemistry creates something new and unique out of careful combinations of chemicals the mastery of mental chemistry...   New Age Pages 354

The Letters of Robert Browning and Elizabeth Barret Barrett 1845-1846 vol II   ISBN: *1-59462-193-4*   **$35.95**
by Robert Browning and Elizabeth Barrett   Biographies Pages 596

Gleanings In Genesis (volume I) *by Arthur W. Pink*   ISBN: *1-59462-130-6*   **$27.45**
Appropriately has Genesis been termed "the seed plot of the Bible" for in it we have, in germ form, almost all of the great doctrines which are afterwards fully developed in the books of Scripture which follow...   Religion/Inspirational Pages 420

The Master Key *by L. W. de Laurence*   ISBN: *1-59462-001-6*   **$30.95**
In no branch of human knowledge has there been a more lively increase of the spirit of research during the past few years than in the study of Psychology, Concentration and Mental Discipline. The requests for authentic lessons in Thought Control, Mental Discipline and...   New Age/Business Pages 422

The Lesser Key Of Solomon Goetia *by L. W. de Laurence*   ISBN: *1-59462-092-X*   **$9.95**
This translation of the first book of the "Lemegton" which is now for the first time made accessible to students of Talismanic Magic was done, after careful collation and edition, from numerous Ancient Manuscripts in Hebrew, Latin, and French...   New Age/Occult Pages 92

Rubaiyat Of Omar Khayyam *by Edward Fitzgerald*   ISBN:*1-59462-332-5*   **$13.95**
Edward Fitzgerald, whom the world has already learned, in spite of his own efforts to remain within the shadow of anonymity, to look upon as one of the rarest poets of the century, was born at Bredfield, in Suffolk, on the 31st of March, 1809. He was the third son of John Purcell...   Music Pages 172

Ancient Law *by Henry Maine*   ISBN: *1-59462-128-4*   **$29.95**
The chief object of the following pages is to indicate some of the earliest ideas of mankind, as they are reflected in Ancient Law, and to point out the relation of those ideas to modern thought.   Religiom/History Pages 452

Far-Away Stories *by William J. Locke*   ISBN: *1-59462-129-2*   **$19.45**
"Good wine needs no bush, but a collection of mixed vintages does. And this book is just such a collection. Some of the stories I do not want to remain buried for ever in the museum files of dead magazine-numbers an author's not unpardonable vanity..."   Fiction Pages 272

Life of David Crockett *by David Crockett*   ISBN: *1-59462-250-7*   **$27.45**
"Colonel David Crockett was one of the most remarkable men of the times in which he lived. Born in humble life, but gifted with a strong will, an indomitable courage, and unremitting perseverance...   Biographies/New Age Pages 424

Lip-Reading *by Edward Nitchie*   ISBN: *1-59462-206-X*   **$25.95**
Edward B. Nitchie, founder of the New York School for the Hard of Hearing, now the Nitchie School of Lip-Reading, Inc, wrote "LIP-READING Principles and Practice". The development and perfecting of this meritorious work on lip-reading was an undertaking...   How-to Pages 400

A Handbook of Suggestive Therapeutics, Applied Hypnotism, Psychic Science   ISBN: *1-59462-214-0*   **$24.95**
by Henry Munro   Health/New Age/Health/Self-help Pages 376

A Doll's House: and Two Other Plays *by Henrik Ibsen*   ISBN: *1-59462-112-8*   **$19.95**
Henrik Ibsen created this classic when in revolutionary 1848 Rome. Introducing some striking concepts in playwriting for the realist genre, this play has been studied the world over.   Fiction/Classics/Plays 308

The Light of Asia *by sir Edwin Arnold*   ISBN: *1-59462-204-3*   **$13.95**
In this poetic masterpiece, Edwin Arnold describes the life and teachings of Buddha. The man who was to become known as Buddha to the world was born as Prince Gautama of India but he rejected the worldly riches and abandoned the reigns of power when...   Religion/History/Biographies Pages 170

The Complete Works of Guy de Maupassant *by Guy de Maupassant*   ISBN: *1-59462-157-8*   **$16.95**
"For days and days, nights and nights, I had dreamed of that first kiss which was to consecrate our engagement, and I knew not on what spot I should put my lips..."   Fiction/Classics Pages 240

The Art of Cross-Examination *by Francis L. Wellman*   ISBN: *1-59462-309-0*   **$26.95**
Written by a renowned trial lawyer, Wellman imparts his experience and uses case studies to explain how to use psychology to extract desired information through questioning.   How-to/Science/Reference Pages 408

Answered or Unanswered? *by Louisa Vaughan*   ISBN: *1-59462-248-5*   **$10.95**
Miracles of Faith in China   Religion Pages 112

The Edinburgh Lectures on Mental Science (1909) *by Thomas*   ISBN: *1-59462-008-3*   **$11.95**
This book contains the substance of a course of lectures recently given by the writer in the Queen Street Hall, Edinburgh. Its purpose is to indicate the Natural Principles governing the relation between Mental Action and Material Conditions...   New Age/Psychology Pages 148

Ayesha *by H. Rider Haggard*   ISBN: *1-59462-301-5*   **$24.95**
Verily and indeed it is the unexpected that happens! Probably if there was one person upon the earth from whom the Editor of this, and of a certain previous history, did not expect to hear again...   Classics Pages 380

Ayala's Angel *by Anthony Trollope*   ISBN: *1-59462-352-X*   **$29.95**
The two girls were both pretty, but Lucy who was twenty-one who supposed to be simple and comparatively unattractive, whereas Ayala was credited, as her Bombwhat romantic name might show, with poetic charm and a taste for romance. Ayala when her father died was nineteen...   Fiction Pages 484

The American Commonwealth *by James Bryce*   ISBN: *1-59462-286-8*   **$34.45**
An interpretation of American democratic political theory. It examines political mechanics and society from the perspective of Scotsman James Bryce   Politics Pages 572

Stories of the Pilgrims *by Margaret P. Pumphrey*   ISBN: *1-59462-116-0*   **$17.95**
This book explores pilgrims religious oppression in England as well as their escape to Holland and eventual crossing to America on the Mayflower, and their early days in New England...   History Pages 268

QTY

The Fasting Cure *by Sinclair Upton*   ISBN: *1-59462-222-1* **$13.95**
*In the Cosmopolitan Magazine for May, 1910, and in the Contemporary Review (London) for April, 1910, I published an article dealing with my experi-
ences in fasting. I have written a great many magazine articles, but never one which attracted so much attention... New Age/Self Help/Health Pages 164*

Hebrew Astrology *by Sepharial*   ISBN: *1-59462-308-2* **$13.45**
*In these days of advanced thinking it is a matter of common observation that we have left many of the old landmarks behind and that we are now pressing
forward to greater heights and to a wider horizon than that which represented the mind-content of our progenitors...   Astrology Pages 144*

Thought Vibration or The Law of Attraction in the Thought World   ISBN: *1-59462-127-6* **$12.95**
by William Walker Atkinson   *Psychology/Religion Pages 144*

Optimism *by Helen Keller*   ISBN: *1-59462-108-X* **$15.95**
*Helen Keller was blind, deaf, and mute since 19 months old, yet famously learned how to overcome these handicaps, communicate with the world, and
spread her lectures promoting optimism. An inspiring read for everyone...   Biographies/Inspirational Pages 84*

Sara Crewe *by Frances Burnett*   ISBN: *1-59462-360-0* **$9.45**
*In the first place, Miss Minchin lived in London. Her home was a large, dull, tall one, in a large, dull square, where all the houses were alike, and all the
sparrows were alike, and where all the door-knockers made the same heavy sound...   Childrens/Classic Pages 88*

The Autobiography of Benjamin Franklin *by Benjamin Franklin*   ISBN: *1-59462-135-7* **$24.95**
*The Autobiography of Benjamin Franklin has probably been more extensively read than any other American historical work, and no other book of its kind
has had such ups and downs of fortune. Franklin lived for many years in England, where he was agent...   Biographies/History Pages 332*

Name	
Email	
Telephone	
Address	
City, State ZIP	

☐ **Credit Card**   ☐ **Check / Money Order**

Credit Card Number	
Expiration Date	
Signature	

*Please Mail to: Book Jungle
PO Box 2226
Champaign, IL 61825*
or Fax to: 630-214-0564

ORDERING INFORMATION

web*: www.bookjungle.com*
email*: sales@bookjungle.com*
fax*: 630-214-0564*
mail*: Book Jungle PO Box 2226 Champaign, IL 61825*
or PayPal *to sales@bookjungle.com*

Please contact us for bulk discounts

DIRECT-ORDER TERMS

**20% Discount if You Order
Two or More Books**
Free Domestic Shipping!
Accepted: Master Card, Visa,
Discover, American Express